Elizabeth

Marshall

Thomas

Illustrated by

Andrew Davidson

Certain ❧ Poor ❧ Shepherds

A Christmas Tale

SIMON & SCHUSTER

SIMON & SCHUSTER
Rockefeller Center
1230 Avenue of the Americas
New York, NY 10020

SIMON & SCHUSTER and colophon are registered
trademarks of Simon & Schuster Inc.

Illustrations © 1996 by Andrew Davidson

Designed by Pei Loi Koay

Manufactured in the United States of America

1   3   5   7   9   10   8   6   4   2

Library of Congress Cataloging-in-Publication Data
Thomas, Elizabeth Marshall.
Certain poor shepherds : a Christmas tale / Elizabeth Marshall Thomas.
p. cm
1. Jesus Christ—Nativity—Fiction. 2. Animals—Fiction.
3. Christmas stories. I. Title.
PS3570.H56253C47 1996
813'.54—dc20 96-34263
CIP

ISBN 0-684-83313-1

To Sy

Come thou, Einion's Yellow One,
Stray Horns, the Particoloured Lake Cow,
And the hornless Dodyn,
Arise, come home.

—FROM *THE STRAY COW*, A WELSH FOLKTALE

Certain

Poor

Shepherds

On the first Christmas, so say the Christians, a redeemer was born to save our kind from the consequences of our greed, waste, pride, cruelty, and arrogance. No redeemer appeared for the animals; however, none was needed. The animals were much the same then as they are now, just as God made them, perfect according to his plan. Perhaps that is why Christ is sometimes portrayed as an animal—simple and humble, a sacrifice, a lamb.

As a result, the Nativity made little difference to most animals. It didn't do them any harm, but—except for one occasion, when Jesus rode a local donkey and thereby marked its race with the holy sign of the cross—it didn't do them any good, either.

There were, however, some exceptions. A few flocks of migrating birds on their way from the coast of the Black Sea to the flooded marshes of the Nile found the star of Bethlehem so powerful that they flew toward it and thus went east when they should have gone south. But that was because their leaders were inexperienced. Eventually they got their bearings and continued on to their wintering grounds. The detour made them late, but otherwise no harm was done.

Also, on the way to Bethlehem, Joseph's donkey noted some succulent prickly pears, but he was not allowed to stop for these delicacies, and when he passed by on the way back, the pears were gone. Someone else had eaten them. And the cows whose manger was taken by Mary had to eat their hay off the floor where, with all the human activity, some got kicked out of reach by passing feet. But these were minor disappointments, the likes of which the animals were used to and soon forgot.

There were, however, a few animals who were profoundly influenced by the events in Bethlehem on that first Christmas. The Nativity—or rather, the circumstances surrounding it—changed their lives forever. This is their story.

One

The story begins on a cold upland pasture where coarse grass and scrub cedar grew. The hour was midnight, the day was the first of winter, and the year of our Lord was zero. On that night a white goat, Ima, and a huge gray short-haired sheepdog, Lila, were keeping watch over a small flock of young sheep.

The sheep were sleeping, protected from the wind in a thicket of cedar whose sweet smell was filling their heads with dreams and their wool with a delicate odor. But the goat, Ima, was not sleeping. She lay on folded legs in the shelter of a nearby boulder, her face raised to the sky. Now and then she would test the night air for scent that might mean danger, but also for scent that might mean another goat or goats, anyone of her own kind. None ever came, but she hoped anyway. Ima was lonely.

Because Ima was intelligent and experienced and had learned, from her mother and aunts, everything a goat needs to know about living in the hills, she was forced by her master, who lived in the valley below, to stay with his young sheep as their guardian. He trusted her to bring them to wild pastures where the best grass grew, he trusted her to know the herbs that would help the young sheep if they were sick, and he trusted her to watch the comings and goings of the birds and the deer so she could find water hidden in the rocks—the secret springs and pools where she could lead his sheep to drink. Ima did all that and more, more than her master ever knew. He never knew, for instance, that his own life had been saved by Ima once, when he was moving his sheep across some rugged hills to a new pasture. Ima had heard the deep, threatening roar of the hilltop cracking and had rushed the sheep out of the way of a rockslide. The master had run after his sheep to try to stop them, which put him beyond the rocks that suddenly came cascading down.

Just as the squeaks of bats are too high for people to hear, so the voices of the hills are too deep. The master didn't realize that his goat ran because she was heeding a warning, and he never realized why he hadn't been crushed. Nevertheless he knew he'd been lucky, and later he sacrificed one of the sheep to thank God for his escape. Actually, the worst danger to Ima had not been from the rocks but from her master himself, because at first it had crossed his mind to sacrifice *her*. Goats were less valuable than sheep. But he had only the one goat and needed her to be his shepherd, so at the last minute he offered God another animal, and Ima went on leading the survivors to water and pasture and medicinal plants.

More she couldn't do. She couldn't save the sheep or even herself from the wolves and the wild cats who roamed the hills at night. That duty fell to the other shepherd, the warrior sheepdog Lila, who that night was curled beside the goat in the shelter of the boulder, out of the cold night wind. Lila's chin lay on her crossed front paws but her eyes were open. She was resting, but at the same time alert. Lila too was lonely, and she liked to feel the warm goat's body through her fur.

Comforted by the big dog's presence, Ima began to chew her cud, a task she saved for her off-duty hours. The dog listened to the familiar crunching of the wise goat's jaws. The night wind turned and blew from the east, and the dog, as was her custom when the wind changed, raised her nose into it, searching it for whatever news it carried. Just then she heard a gulp and a short bleat, a startled call from Ima. At the same time, she felt her hair tickle as if before a thunderstorm. What was it? The dog looked up.

Insistently, Ima called again, a quick, short bleat of puzzlement that ended on a rising note, like a question. Then she stood up. Lila felt a sudden chill as the goat's

The warrior sheepdog Lila that night was curled beside the goat.

body moved away from hers. She too stood up, lifting her nose into the east wind to learn what might have startled Ima. But the wind held only grass and cedar. Wondering if she should be alarmed, puzzled by the gentle prickling of her skin, Lila followed Ima's gaze and noticed something bright above the line of cedars on the eastern horizon.

It was a very bright star. Curious, Lila watched it. She knew the night sky from a lifetime underneath it, but she had never before seen this star, or, for that matter, so big a star. The two shepherds exchanged a glance. They saw on each other's faces expressions of both puzzlement and wonder, but not of fear. Wolves frightened them. Their master in the valley frightened them, at least when he was angry. Bad storms frightened them. But not a star. Interested, the dog and the goat waited to see if something more would happen.

But nothing did. The star stayed fixed, radiating its power through the cold night sky. The dog gently lifted her nose and tested for scent a third time. She was just a dog, and she didn't expect to understand everything, but when something unusual happened she knew to search the wind to see what she could learn from it. It was her business to understand as much as she could, the better to serve her master. Sure enough, this time in the east wind she found a strange new odor, a pure, clear scent halfway between honey and water, halfway between rock and cedar, strongest toward the east in front of her, weaker to her left and right, and hardly detectable behind her. It was, she realized, coming from the star.

Again she sampled the remarkable odor. This time she found power in it—a great deal of power. Now the goat joined her, raising her upper lip to let the scent flow over her gums. Soon both animals had found the odor. They exchanged a glance, each hoping to learn what the other thought. But neither knew what to make of it.

By this time the movements of the dog and goat on the rocky ledge had awakened the sheep who, seeing that their shepherds were watching something, moved away from the warmth of the thicket to a bare, windy rock where they too could see the sky. All the animals realized that a new and powerful star had risen above the eastern horizon.

The night was windy and the hillside was cold. Even so, rather than seek shelter, the animals gazed at the star for a very long time, feeling its charged light lift their hair, as charged air does before a storm. They would look at the star, then at one another. But no matter how long they did this, they couldn't understand it. Whatever it was, though, like lightning or rockslides or fire or the night wind, it was strong. Even the animals knew that.

In time the young sheep grew uncomfortably cold and crept back to their places in the thicket. Ima too lay down again behind the boulder, folding first her front legs, then her hind legs, and resumed chewing her cud.

Lila selected a likely spot beside her, circled a few times, and sank down to rest.

Influenced by the star, all the animals dreamed. Lila dreamed of a fire—the hearth in her master's household. She dreamed she was curled by that fire, and in the curve of her body were four tender pups. She dreamed of their warm mouths on her nipples and their soft, sweet-smelling bodies against her skin. Then, in her dream, she knew she had to get up to tend the sheep in their high pasture. She went because it was her duty to go, and she was gone a long time. When she got back, she saw in her dream that her puppies were gone. In vain she tried to find them. As she desperately searched, rushing here and there and crying, the master and his wife quietly looked on. In her dream, Lila felt they knew what had happened. With her eyes she begged them. In her dream, she saw that the two people understood what she wanted. And so, in her dream, they put their hands into a basin of water, lifted out the four limp puppies, and laid them on the floor. Overjoyed, Lila licked them dry, and soon they were once again awake and safe in the curve of her body.

By the light of the strong star the goat, Ima, dreamed of a huge, dark fold where food was so scarce she ate the wood the fold was made of. But it was the fold where she was born, and for that reason she was happy. With her were her mother, her father, her aunts, her cousins, and her brothers and sisters. But suddenly, in the dream, a strange man strode into the fold, grabbed her by one of her horns, and dragged her to him. She fought, but he put a noose around her neck, tied the other end of the rope to the saddle of a donkey, and dragged her miles away to his stable. She fought every step of the way. Once again, in her dream, she felt the choking rope around her neck, the suffocating dust of the trail in her nostrils, and the terror and confusion in her heart.

When they arrived at her new home and her new master finally let her go, she saw that no other goats were there to greet her, just some young sheep. In her dream she knew she should live among these sheep and lead them. In her dream she remembered how she tried to find food and water and to learn her way in the strange new countryside, the wild hillsides near her master's fold. Wherever she went, the young sheep followed. They were always on her heels, always hungry, always begging. In her dream they annoyed her. When she found food, they hurried in to share.

Suddenly, in her dream, she heard her mother call. It seemed to Ima that her mother wanted to help her. With the bothersome sheep trotting after her, she hurried toward the voice. At first, no one was there. But suddenly the dream changed, and Ima was back in her first fold, standing among her kin, waiting for the shepherd to open the gate to let them graze in the familiar hills of home.

The young sheep also dreamed by the light of the new star. Their dreams were entirely happy, with no sad parts to them, and were of their shepherds, the goat and the dog. One sheep dreamed of following Ima down to a plowed field where she found freshly sprouting wheat and ate her fill. Another sheep dreamed of the silhouette of Lila standing tall against the night sky, keeping him from harm.

Toward morning, hunger woke the sheep as usual. They called their greetings to one another, waking their shepherds. Remembering, the dog and the goat looked at the sky and saw that the star was still there. Soon the animals heard footsteps on the trail that led up from the valley. The master was coming, bringing food in a basin for Lila as he did every morning when Lila was out with the sheep. Quickly putting her nose in the air, Lila learned that the basin contained curds and bread crusts. Rejoicing at the prospect of her daily meal, she watched her master materialize in the starlight, a short, strong, bearded man who wore sandals and a rough, woolen garment tied at the waist with a rope. When he saw his animals he stopped and emptied the bowl over a flat stone.

Ima happened to be near the stone, so she sniffed at the food as it dropped. Every day Ima ate her fill of grass and leaves, of buds and branches, and she never ate curds or table scraps, so when she learned what the master had brought, she looked away, uninterested. Lila, on the other hand, could not eat the plants of the upland pasture, and was so big that the small amount of food her master brought was never quite enough. She was always hungry, and she didn't like to see anyone, not even Ima, so near her meager ration. Giving Ima a hard look, she snapped up her food instantly. Too quickly, it was gone. Very humbly, Lila looked at her master, her head down, her ears low, her tail faintly wagging, thanking him for the food but also wondering if by chance there was still a bit more in his bowl. Ordinarily her master didn't pay much attention to what she wanted, but that morning he put the bowl on the ground. Quickly, Lila cleaned it with her tongue, then looked again at her master to see what he made of the star.

At first he didn't seem to notice it. A little while later he glanced at it as if its presence had registered for the first time, and he seemed to study it briefly, as if it puzzled him too. But Lila's master wasn't much interested in puzzles. He stifled a yawn, wrapped his garment tight against the cold, picked up his bowl, and glanced right and left to learn the weather. Then he whistled twice, meaning that Lila was to bring the sheep and follow. She hurried to obey, rushing among the sheep to get them moving, then zigzagging behind them to keep them in an orderly group around her master's legs.

The sheep did well that morning. Lila was pleased with the way they hurried to do as she directed. It was almost too dark to see, but she made out their woolly rumps all grouped together, the way sheep ought to look, in a flock that was orderly and tight, with the solitary goat up in front beside the master. Good. But the obedience of the sheep did not relax Lila's vigilance. As she padded silently behind the sheep down the dark trail, she trained her ears on the rhythmic clacking of feet on the stony ground while her eyes scanned the mass of woolly rumps. She needed to know that nobody was running too fast or going wide of the group or lagging.

Yet if her eyes were on the sheep, her splendid nose was meanwhile studying the multitude of odors that rose from the earth, or clung to the bushes, or hung overhead in the cold morning air. She knew each tree and shrub and bush. She knew them by their kind—the cedars smelled different from the olive trees, for instance. But she also knew each plant by its family. All of the cedars at the top of the trail were the children, grandchildren, or tiny, sprouting great-grandchildren of one huge, wind-bent cedar that grew on the ridge of the hill, and their odor was different—slightly different but different never-theless—from the odors of the cedars near the bottom of the trail. These cedars were the children of three different parents, none of whom were living. Two were stumps, cut down for firewood by Lila's master. The third had vanished, burned in a brushfire. And one lonely cedar was related to none of the others. Its seed must have been dropped by a bird. All this Lila's sensitive nose had told her. Beyond that, though, she also knew each tree by its personal odor. Since trees don't move, these scents were fixed, like landmarks, so Lila always knew exactly where she was on the trail, even if her eyes and ears were busy with the sheep.

She also could tell who else had used the trail. Her master's scent, for instance, still hung heavy from his walk up the hill. Despite the cold, he had been perspiring; his sweat smelled of the curds he had eaten before he came. She also found the scent of the food he had carried. On its way up the hill it had perfumed the bushes. Lila sighed, feeling a little sad to think that this food existed no longer, but had already been eaten, that only the scent remained.

A bit farther she found the musky odor of a fox. Lila knew him—he had a den on that hillside. He was too small to bother the sheep, but even so, Lila didn't like him and would chase him when they met. She looked at the back of her master's head and shoulders as he plodded down the trail. He didn't seem interested in the fox, but she had expected that. His indifference to the odors they passed had long ago ceased to surprise her. A bit later she caught the odor of another fox. A stranger! Lila was just beginning to study this fox when suddenly her nostrils filled with another new scent, which raised the hair all along her spine. Streaming across the trail on the cold east wind was the acrid, frightening scent of a full-grown male lynx! Lila's eyes flew wide as she caught his sign very strongly on one of the bushes by the trail. He had sprayed it! He had claimed it! Worse yet, he was still nearby.

Surely the master would react to this, thought Lila. Surely he wouldn't just ignore such a dangerous, proud animal claiming a place so near his sheep! Surely the master would want Lila to learn more about the big cat, to find him, to chase him up a tree and keep him there, displaying long teeth and much ferocity below, so he'd see the sheep were protected. But the master didn't seem to notice even this terrible thing. Head down and shoulders sagging, he plodded onward, passing right through the threatening stream of lynx odor as if nothing were wrong.

The goat noticed, though, and shot Lila a worried glance just to be sure that the dog was still there to protect her. And the sheep noticed. These youngsters didn't know much, but they knew enough to be frightened by the strong odor of a large wild cat. With anxious bleats they crowded into one another, looking nervously over their shoulders. Lila had to nip some of them to keep them together.

But even this her master didn't notice. Lila saw that he was going to do nothing about the lynx except to ignore him, to let him prowl and spray wherever he liked. And so the group walked steadily downhill, the master leading, Ima fearful, the sheep confused, and Lila deeply disappointed and a bit angry at her master for preventing her from doing what was right.

The sky in the east was milky gray, Lila noticed, the first true light to herald the fiery sun. This made her happy. She looked forward to the sun and its warmth after the bitter night. Then she remembered the new star and looked up. The star was still bright even though the other stars were fading. But when Lila checked it again a few minutes later, more daylight had gathered, and the new star too had turned pale.

Then, for the first time, the dog felt anxious. The extraordinary star was leaving, off to join the other stars in their places behind the sun. If its power had belonged to a dog or a person, she would have wanted to follow it. She looked quickly at her master, hoping that he would notice what was happening to the star. As usual he trudged on as if nothing were different, quickening his pace as the trail became level. But behind him, the sheep noticed that the star would soon be gone. Sensing their shepherds' anxiety, they tried to hurry off in its direction, and Lila had all she could do to hold them back.

Three

At the edge of the cultivated land, their master stopped. He had brought his animals to a wheat field by a grove of olive trees. The wheat and the olives had long since been harvested, but plenty of rich stubble remained on the ground. He whistled again, a signal for the dog to release the sheep so that they could graze there.

The animals hesitated a moment. They were watching the star grow dim as the sky around it turned blue. Soon it would vanish, and so would their master, and they would be alone. By now, though, Ima and the sheep were hungry. If the star would go, it would go, the young sheep seemed to think, and they spread out to graze. Whistling to his dog to tell her not to follow him, the master turned to leave. So the dog sat down to watch him walk away. The sight only increased the loneliness that she had begun to feel with the fading of the star.

Suddenly Lila's nose was filled with an odor like that of the star, but stronger and more mysterious. Then, overhead, she heard a rush of wings. Startled, she leaped up, expecting to see geese or storks, but was amazed to see, instead, right above her, the wings and bellies of a flock of angels speeding headlong through the air. She barked sharply to alert her master, and he turned back. Very excited, she stood up to be ready for whatever he might ask of her but, as if he didn't notice or care about the angels, who by now were passing right in front of him, he looked at her in an angry manner and bent down to fix his sandal. A strap had broken. He began to tie the two ends back together.

But Ima and the sheep saw what their master could not, and, their jaws slack, their bites of half-chewed grass forgotten on their tongues, they had all stopped still to look at the wonderful sight. Lila barked again, desperate that her master, who habitually ignored most sounds and all odors, should not ignore this too. But her warnings only made him angry. He looked up from his sandal and angrily shouted something. She knew he meant for her to keep quiet and guard the sheep. Crestfallen, she sat down again.

Still, she couldn't take her eyes off the angels. Flying in front were several large ones, who seemed to be the leaders. Faster than swallows they led the others in a circle above the cultivated ground. Suddenly, all swooped low, then, scattering star odor and banking their wings, they swung their bodies upright, extended their feet, and bounced to earth running. A few steps brought them to a halt.

With perfect composure they looked around, took note of one another, then shook out and folded their wings. The action caused the long flight-feathers to rustle. Then, without as much as a nod to one another and with no more than passing glances at the amazed animals, they spread out, squatted down on their haunches, and began to forage through the stubble on the field and under the olive trees around it. Now and then one of the angels would find an olive or a kernel of grain left behind by the harvesters and would toss it into its mouth. They seemed hungry. Some of them wouldn't bother to stand before moving to a new area but would just hitch along, duckwalking to the next furrow and the next bit of food.

Again the dog and the goat exchanged a glance. In the past they had seen angels only rarely, and then only above the highest ridges, where occasionally one would soar overhead, at ease on the rising air. But neither Ima nor Lila had ever seen so many angels all together, and never before so near, and again they looked at their master to see what he made of them.

But he was done with his sandal and was leaving. Just as he would not heed the warning given by a hilltop before a rockslide, or listen to the high calls made by bats on the wing, and just as he would not investigate the scent-mark of a dangerous lynx, so he would not look at angels even though they were all around him. As far as he was concerned, they weren't there.

But sounds too high or low for human ears are nevertheless sounds; odors too faint or pure for human nostrils are nevertheless odors; and beings invisible to human eyes are nevertheless beings. Her master's dense oblivion dismayed Lila. She watched him walk so near a crouching angel that he almost knocked her over. Insensible, he walked to the edge of the field and vanished among the olive trees.

By this time Ima and the sheep had spread out among the angels to enjoy the stubble. The angels continued to forage for grain. Then, as the search took some of them to the edge of the plowed land, a young she-angel gave a joyful cry. The dog and goat saw that she had found an oak tree with acorns. Flying and running, the flock hurried to join her. Some of the angels flew up into the branches and shook the acorns to the ground, where other angels gathered them. The large male angels bit right into the acorns, while the smaller angels found stones and cracked the shells.

Upon noticing this new source of food, Lila cautiously made her way toward the oak tree. She was such a big, dangerous-looking dog that most of the angels grew apprehensive and stopped eating to watch her come. A large male angel flew down out of the tree to stand between the dog and the other angels. But the dog wanted only friendship, and perhaps a share of the food. Humbly she lowered her ears and head and bent her knees, and with faintly wagging tail approached the angels so gently that they saw at once there was nothing to fear. Slowly, respectfully, Lila crept to the male angel and bowed down at his feet.

He gave her some acorns. She had never eaten acorns before, so she sniffed them for a moment, then tried one. She didn't like the bitter taste but thought the meat could be nourishing, and in moments she had bolted them, shells and all. Then she lifted a paw to thank the angel. She was her most charming self, ears low, chin lifted, tail faintly tapping. The angel bent down to scratch her ears, and many of the other angels gathered around.

Far away, Ima, the goat, raised her head and saw the excitement. She realized that whatever Lila and the angels were doing had something to do with food, so, followed by her young sheep, she came trotting in Lila's direction. Most of the angels seemed to like animals, and they welcomed the newcomers with acorns, which sheep and goats love. Ima and her young charges ate greedily,

*Upon noticing this new source of food, Lila cautiously
made her way toward the oak tree.*

jostling one another for space at the acorn pile, and when it was gone they looked around for more. A small sheep who had not been able to push her way into the feast was hand-fed by a young she-angel.

The same angel noticed burs stuck to Lila's haunches, and gently took them off. Lila was grateful, as these burs had prickled her whenever she sat; she had been unsuccessfully biting at them for days. When Lila visited a nearby spring for a drink of the barely moving water, she smelled a frog asleep in its tiny hole nearby, and dug it out and carried it undamaged in her mouth as a gift for the angel. Newly awakened, the frog sat on the angel's hand, blinking and pulsing its throat in terror. Lila had meant for the angel to eat the frog, but instead the angel put it gently down as if giving it its freedom. So Lila ate it.

By now the sun was high and the day was slowly getting warmer, and under the oak tree many of the angels were lying down to sleep. In the grass beyond the tree, Ima and the young sheep also lay down—front legs first—and coughed up their cuds to begin the task of chewing. As Ima had taught them, the sheep lay in a group, but facing out, so that at all times someone was keeping watch in every direction. They were supposed to be vigilant, but in time most of them dozed. The dog dozed too, but didn't sleep deeply. As always, she was ready to wake the moment danger threatened, ready with her white teeth and her brave heart to defend her flock.

The goat, the sheep, and even the angels slept more soundly, knowing that Lila was near.

So passed the winter afternoon. Later the sun went behind the hills in the west, the hills from which the two shepherd animals and their sheep had come. The cold deepened as the night wind rose. The goat led the sheep back to the field to eat more stubble, while the dog nosed through the grass for insects made slow by cold, or for acorns that the angels might have missed. The angels, too, were waking up, shaking out their wings and preening their feathers, getting ready for flight.

When the sky behind the hills turned red with the sunset, the angels began to flock together. Soon they were all within arm's reach of one another, some sitting, some standing, as they watched the darkening eastern sky.

Slowly, faint and pale at first, the star appeared. As the darkness deepened, the star got brighter, its perfume on the wind, its light as charged and brilliant as it had been the night before. The angels faced into the wind and looked expectant. Suddenly some of the larger angels started running, and then, with all the others racing behind them, they spread their wings and, with loud calls and noisily creaking feathers, ran flapping into the sky. By the time the flock had reached the end of the field all the angels were prone, like birds in the air, like swimmers in water, and were building speed. They whirled once around the field to get their bearings, then shot off to the east, straight for the star.

Immediately Lila went bounding after them, but the flock of angels traveled so fast that to keep up was impossible. Very soon the dog saw that the chase was hopeless, and she stopped, discouraged, her ears and tail drooping, to watch them out of sight. The angels, who had been massed at first, were straggling out in a long uneven line, like a flock of geese. The leaders were tracking the star, she realized, using it as a beacon. That fact did not surprise her. Like the kindred cedars along the trail in the hills, the star and the angels shared an odor. They belonged together as one thing. Surely the star was their leader, who had gone on ahead, or who had come from the other side of the world and summoned them.

Strangely lonely, Lila turned to Ima to learn how she was taking this. Ima stood straight and tall, eyes bright, looking after the departing flock. She seemed happy, ready for anything. She turned suddenly to Lila. She even shook her tail and her head as if she were impatient, and danced a few steps on stiff legs toward the east, as if she expected something. Then Lila knew that Ima also felt the pull of the star, that she too wanted to keep up with the angels and not be left behind. Suddenly it seemed clear to her that she and Ima must round up their sheep and go where the star called them.

. . .

Taking their direction from the star, the animals traveled for four nights over hills and through valleys, past olive groves and vineyards, past little settlements where other dogs barked at them. At dawn, when the star faded, they stopped and waited for evening when it showed itself again. Finding food was much easier for the goat and the sheep than it was for Lila, but being a dog, she could fast for a long time. Even so, she managed to find a few morsels. It helped that the animals were following roughly the path of the angels—here and there Lila found faint traces of their odor that had fallen to the ground—because the path led to several food sources. Most foods eaten by the angels were inedible to dogs, but some Lila found nourishing. On the second night, for instance, she caught the scent of figs, and, by the light of a new moon, soon found the tree itself. The figs had been harvested, and the angels had feasted on most of those that were left, shriveled and dry with winter, but they had left some on the ground. The dog ate them. On the third night, in a range of hills so high that the trees along the ridge were bent by the wind, the dog scented carrion, and found the partly eaten carcass of a deer that a lynx had dragged under the shelter of a boulder and covered with leaves. Evidently the carcass had not tempted the angels—they had passed it by—but the dog finished it gladly, every scrap, even cracking the bones and licking out the marrow.

At the end of the fourth night the animals found themselves in a small vineyard such as farmers make outside a village. There the star was directly above them and its scent was strong. They had answered its call. They had come.

Four

B ut what place were they in? And what were they to do? Ima and the tired young sheep knew at once the answer to these questions. Gratefully, they began to munch the grape leaves. Lila watched their white backs moving slowly down the rows of carefully supported vines. But dry grape leaves are not the same thing to a dog that they are to sheep and goats. Listening to the crunching of Ima's jaws and watching her tail shake with pleasure, hungry Lila wished that she too could be fed. In search of food, she raised her nose to catch whatever scents the morning wind might carry.

In westward-drifting air quite high above the cold earth, she found a layer of many scents all mixed together, and realized that she had found the traces of a center of some kind, a place where many animals and people were gathered. She found the smells of filth and spice, of dust and fodder, of moist earth which meant water, and of several other dogs. She also found the star odor, but that did not surprise her. She had been expecting that. She let it pass and investigated some of the others.

Of course, it was the food that most intrigued her. But she couldn't consider the food without also considering the other dogs. In a strange place, a dog never knows what to expect from her own kind. Would the other dogs prevent her from eating? Would she find friendship among them? Would she have to fight? Lila was big enough and strong enough to fight wolves, but still she worried. Her mind's eye saw the village dogs with angry faces and glaring eyes, their hair high, their heads low and menacing, showing all their teeth, ready to band together against a common threat. They'd be on their own ground, too, and she would be a stranger.

Still, the smell of food came from their direction. By now she was painfully hungry and, test the wind as she would, she could find no trace of food in any other quarter. So she decided that, dogs or not, she would follow the promising odor.

She glanced over her shoulder for a glimpse of Ima. She wanted the goat to know that she would be gone for a while. The white backs of the browsing animals were scattered all through the vineyard, but at last Lila distinguished the goat from the others. Head down, Ima was busy eating and would not notice her. Lila looked up at the star, by now almost lost in the morning sky. She felt very much alone. And so, she knew, would Ima when she found her gone. But she always came back to Ima, as Ima had always come back to her. Whenever Ima returned, Lila would learn from the smell of the goat's feet or legs or mantle where she'd been and why she'd gone there. She knew that Ima, even without a sense of smell as discerning as her own, trusted her implicitly. With a last look over her shoulder at her oblivious friend, Lila trotted off toward Bethlehem.

Five

Ima looked up from browsing and found herself alone. Or so she felt. The sheep were there, yes, all eating busily, but to Ima they meant responsibility, not companionship. And without Lila the entire burden of their care fell on her. She looked sourly at the day ahead, knowing it would be filled with young sheep nudging, needing food or water or shelter from the wind or a place to chew their cuds. But as she watched them raise their heads to look at her after every few bites, she could see how anxious they were to keep her in sight, and how relieved they seemed to find her still with them, and her heart softened. She remembered how very young they had been when they first came into her care, just lambs, really. Like her, they had been taken too soon from their mothers. Their dependence was irritating, but it wasn't their fault. The young sheep should be with their mothers, but they were not; that was all. Ima understood about that.

Ima remembered the other goats, her family, in the fold where she was born. She remembered her mother's face and golden eyes. Ima often thought of her family, even though the picture she held of them in her mind's eye only made her more lonely. She remembered how pleasant it had been to live with her own kind and wished that at least one other goat could join her flock. A goat could share her life in a way that a dog could not. If the other goat went away for a time, Ima would know where and why. And a goat would understand about plants. Lila didn't understand about poisonous leaves, Ima had discovered, or about short grass being better and easier to eat than long grass. Lila didn't even seem to remember where the best grass was. Also, instead of eating it when someone else found it, Lila would lie down in it, trampling it first with her feet. Then it struck Ima that patches of grass grew here and there around the vineyard, and that Lila might be sleeping in one of those patches at that very moment.

A large, spreading olive tree stood near the edge of the vineyard. Ima went to it and hopped up onto the lowest branch. Then she hopped to the next branch and the next until she was high off the ground. And indeed there was something curled up in the grass, she noticed—not

Lila but a she-angel, and a young one, too. Her eyes were shut, and she had covered herself with her wings. Even so, Ima recognized her—she was the angel who had made sure that every young sheep got a share of acorns, the angel who had pulled the burs from Lila's fur. But something was wrong with her now. Even from a distance the angel looked pale and sick to Ima.

Why was the angel alone? Like sheep and goats, angels should travel together, Ima thought. Then it came to her that a sick angel, like a sick sheep, would most likely straggle along at the rear of the flock, and might fall far behind the others. The others might not even know she was gone. The angels had no shepherding dog to look after them and keep them all together. They were forced to do the best they could on their own.

Ima sighed. Just when her responsibilities seemed too heavy to bear, another one appeared, and a sick one at that. But what could she do? She couldn't just leave the angel lying there. So she climbed down out of the tree and approached the poor creature.

Alone in the grass, the sleeping angel seemed even younger than she had before, and very fragile with her delicate feathers and thin arms and legs. A very faint, mild star fragrance wafted from her, but at the moment she reminded Ima less of the mighty force that surrounded the star than of an orphaned sheep badly in need of someone's care. Stepping boldly up to her, Ima sniffed her breath. The angel stirred in her sleep and seemed about to wake. Ima drew back, but not before she caught a whiff of poison.

As often happened when she found a rare odor, Ima remembered her mother and her aunts. It was they who had taught her the odors of the poisons and of the plants that made them. The angel had eaten the berries of such a plant. Ima had seen several on the journey. She hadn't touched them, of course, and she had guided the young sheep away from them so that they hadn't touched them either. Perhaps the angels hadn't known to leave the plants alone, or this angel had happened to eat a few berries by accident. At any rate, Ima believed that for every sickness there was a remedy, and she thought of a certain spiny plant that would help the angel feel better.

The angel woke, feeling Ima's breath tickle her skin; and recognizing the goat immediately, she put an arm around her neck. But the angel smelled strongly of the poison, and Ima decided that rather than wait any longer, she should bring the invalid to one of the healing plants.

Finding these plants would not be difficult, Ima knew. They were common enough because only goats ate them. Other creatures could not tolerate the spines. For the same reason, few creatures other than goats knew their healthful properties. Head high, Ima stared at the angel, looking alert and a little restless to show that she wanted the angel to follow her.

The angel seemed to understand, and she stood up. Ima led the way, the sheep trailing her, the angel at her side with a hand on Ima's back, a hand as light as a flower petal, a dry mimosa leaf.

But on four legs to the angel's two, Ima walked faster than the angel, and the angel didn't feel well enough to keep up. After a few hurried steps she suddenly placed both palms on Ima's back and, giving a little leap, sat on her, legs to one side.

Aghast at such a liberty, Ima stopped in her tracks. Anyone else would instantly have been bucked off over Ima's horns. But the angel seemed as light as a bird, as the air almost. With her delicate fingers she slowly began to comb the crest of Ima's neck. The combing was pleasant and Ima started walking again.

Surrounded by the sheep, they came at last to a patch of the spiny plants not very far from the vineyard. Ima looked at the plants, then at the angel. The sheep crowded in to see what Ima had found. A few of them tasted the plants then spat them out again, stung by the spines. The angel seemed puzzled. Even sheep won't eat these plants, her expression seemed to say. So Ima nipped a few spines off one plant, making a smooth place on the leaf. Again she looked at the angel. Cautiously the angel picked up the leaf and nibbled a few bites. Ima lay down, front legs first, coughing up her cud to show the angel that she was going to stay for a while. Some of the sheep lay down nearby, but most of them hurried about in search of something more edible. The angel sat down next to Ima, an arm over her shoulders, and ate a little more of the

The angel seemed as light as a bird, as the air almost.

healing leaf. The smell of poison was fading. The angel looked much better already. And that was lucky because, unwittingly, the sheep had trampled and broken the other plants, so that none were left standing. For a second time that day, Ima sighed.

Six

When Lila left Ima in the vineyard she followed a dusty, well-worn track that seemed to lead her toward the scent of food. The track became wider and more dusty as it neared the town, and Lila began to notice the marks of other dogs on stones and the walls of houses. She checked these marks very carefully and found they were made by both male dogs and female dogs, some of high rank. That worried her. She was also disheartened to learn that all the marks, including those of the high-ranking dogs, contained a bitter scent that told of hunger. The dogs here did not eat much, she realized.

One dog in particular worried Lila. A male, he seemed to be the leader. His mark lay over almost every other mark and on fresh surfaces too, as if he claimed every-thing and outranked everybody. From the height of his mark, Lila realized that he was not as big as she was, but he was surely powerful nevertheless, and certainly if it came to a fight he would have others fighting on his side. He would, she realized, be a formidable enemy. If he didn't want her around, she knew, she'd have serious trouble.

Even so, her hunger and the suggestion of food, how-ever unpromising, kept Lila walking. As the sun rose she reached the edge of town and, not wanting to confront another dog before she had to, she chose an inconspicu-ous pathway, a narrow alley between plaster walls. It hap-pened to lead to the main square.

Lila had never before been in a town or a city, and she wasn't ready for what she found there. She wasn't ready to see so many houses, or such a crowd of people gath-ered near a large inn on the other side of the square. Within the walls of the inn was a stable, apparently the center of all the activity despite its run-down state. Doves and sparrows whirled in flocks around the houses or perched on the low walls that enclosed the flat roofs. And angels, including some of the angels Lila had met in the wheat field, sat in rows on the roofs. Other angels flew about as if looking for somewhere to settle. No sooner would an angel leave a space than another angel would plunk down there.

Lila had never seen so much activity. Feeling shy and

not a little frightened, she squeezed into a narrow space between two houses where she could watch what went on while remaining as inconspicuous as possible.

The little village of Bethlehem was never meant to hold so many people. For days and even weeks before, people who had nothing to do with the star had been arriving. Following an empire-wide decree from the Roman treasury, people were returning to the provinces of their birth to discuss their taxes with the authorities. Many of them stayed in Bethlehem, one of the few towns with a decent inn, and a lot less expensive than the larger City of David. And then the star, with its message of hope, had drawn pilgrims from miles around. Tradesmen with their families had come from nearby villages, shepherds with their sheep had come from the hills, and a caravan of traders, seeing the star while camped in the desert, had made a detour. Taxpayers had filled the inn even before the Nativity, and by the fourth day after the star appeared, every house in town had pilgrims in it. Even the village elders were busy playing host.

To a dog fresh from the country, the little town seemed daunting. The cloud of odors that enveloped Lila was so strong and so confusing that she couldn't at first make out what she was sensing. Although the sun had barely risen, traders had set up stands and were already selling dates and oranges. The stronger beggars had seized the best corners from the weaker beggars and were beseeching alms from passersby. The townspeople were selling bread and poultry—mostly chickens and locally caught doves—and water carriers with dripping waterskins were preparing to sell water by the cup to thirsty travelers who didn't know where the spring was.

Suddenly Lila was startled by strange, loud calls and bellows. Down an alleyway came an enormous, long-necked animal the likes of which she had never seen before. Its back was humped like a hill, its sneering upper lip was split like a hare's, it swayed when it walked, and it reeked so strongly that Lila had to sneeze. With its saddlebags scraping the sides of the houses, it advanced slowly and deliberately through the alley, gazing at the second-story windows with scornful eyes. Lila's lips wrinkled in fear, and she shrank even closer to the wall.

At the sight of the dog the big animal groaned, startling Lila so much that she couldn't help but give a worried bark. The camel, for that is what it was, lifted its chin and spat at her, then without breaking stride raised its long, strong foreleg and gave her a sideways kick that caught her in the ribs. She cried out. One of the camel drivers cursed and, squeezing past the camel, raised his whip and dealt Lila a heavy blow that sent her screaming into the square, where yet another driver went after her with his stick.

Terrified, Lila squeezed between a barrel and a wall. From there she could hear more groaning and spitting, more creaking of saddles. Fearing that one of the drivers would see her and hit her again, she shrank as far back as

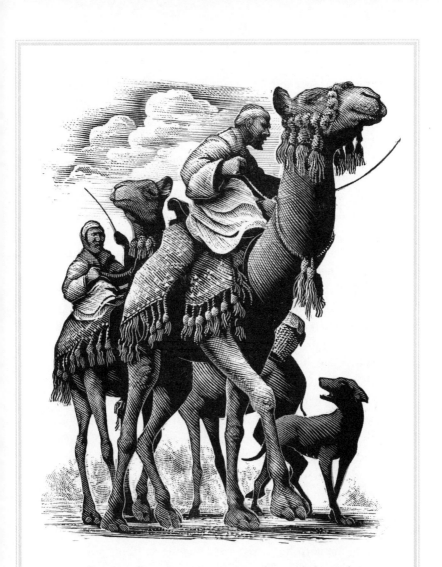

*Down an alleyway came an enormous, long-necked animal
the likes of which she had never seen before.*

she could, peeking out again just in time to see another camel following the first, and then another and another, eight in all, three with large, bearded men riding in their saddles. Other men walked before and behind.

To Lila the three bearded men on the camels seemed important—quite different from the camel drivers. Not only were these three riding the camels rather than trotting along beside them, but their manner was quiet and sure, rather than angry and excited. Also, they held themselves proudly, with their backs straight and their heads high. They didn't look alike—one had black skin and white hair, one had brown skin and black hair, and one had white skin and brown hair—but they acted alike. Their faces were grave—they seemed to have much on their minds. None of them deigned to look around at the village. Lila knew that they must be the masters of the camels, and of the other men too.

And what camels to master! Filling the narrow alley with their bodies, filling the air with their powerful odor, their groans and squeals and the loud creaking of their saddles, they seemed as big as mountains. The drivers worked their way among them with much shouting and cursing and, as each camel emerged from the alley, rounded it up with the others in the village square, which they crowded. There, moaning and muttering, the camels were made to lie down, first kneeling in front, pitching the three riders forward, then reluctantly, after many curses, folding their hind legs, jerking the riders straight up with a jolt as the haunches hit the ground. Ignoring the spitting and the moaning, one of the drivers tied a rope around each camel's bent foreleg so it couldn't stand up again. The three important men then slid down from their saddles and, pausing briefly to distribute some coins among the beggars who clustered around them, went into the stable.

It was not the sight of the camels that most amazed Lila, however. Her remarkable nose told her that much of the baggage consisted of food—a long-dead sheep, lentils, raisins, chickpeas, sweet bread, dates, olives, and oranges—splendid, fragrant food that few dogs ever see, let alone taste. Lila had never even imagined so much food all in one place at one time. Certainly her master never ate so richly. Feeling very humble in the presence of these dizzying odors, but well knowing that she and her hunger would not be welcome here, Lila swallowed hard. Her mouth was watering painfully.

Then suddenly she caught the scent of cat. The scent came from a huge wicker basket that was strapped to the side of a kneeling camel. Spotted fur was sticking through the weave. First making sure that the drivers with the sticks and whips were not watching, Lila approached this interesting fur. Inside the basket an enormous lanky female cat lay curled—a cheetah.

Lila had seen a cheetah only once before; it had been ambling along the far side of a plain where Lila and her master were herding sheep. At the sight of Lila, the cheetah had run away. The cheetah in the basket might have liked to run too, but since she couldn't, she bravely hissed at Lila's investigating nose. Yet her folded ears, her worried eyes, and the nervous twitching of her tail through a little hole in the wicker belied her show of courage. Lila would have liked to inspect the tail, but when she tried, the cheetah turned to face her, and the tail withdrew.

Circling the camel, Lila found that it was also carrying a second, smaller basket. She investigated this basket too, and found that it held a huge bird, an enormous golden eagle. The basket and the camel's flank underneath were white with droppings, and inside, the bird crouched low, his wings partly opened. His eyes were yellow like the cheetah's, and he hissed and snapped his terrible beak when the dog came near. But unlike the cheetah, the eagle betrayed no hesitation, no doubts or fears. Everything about him made it clear that if he had to struggle with a dog or any other animal, or with any person or any thing, he'd win. The sureness of victory that blazed from his eyes dampened Lila's curiosity. More than a little unsettled, and still fearful of the drivers with their sticks and whips, she began to slink away.

Just then she heard a sharp, furious bark—a challenge—and she looked up to see a thin, leggy, short-haired dog, ears raised, head and tail high, standing boldly at the edge of the village square. This was the moment she had feared.

• • •

There was nothing for it. Faced with a strange dog, Lila knew she would have to stand her ground. Bravely, because she suspected that in the alleys were other dogs who would rush to the stranger's side the moment they heard fighting, Lila leveled her neck, widened her eyes, bared her teeth, and raised all the fur on her body. She then began a slow, stiff-legged advance upon the stranger. So intent was she upon the strange dog that she passed near the nose of a camel without noticing that he reached out to bite. Nor did she notice a flock of doves that flew up at her approach. Lila saw only the bold eyes and firm stance of the stranger, and realized that this dog would give no ground.

After a few paces, Lila stopped and challenged him with hard eyes to make the next move. So he fixed her with his own stare, and on his own stiff legs strode forward. Lila tried to steel herself for the fight that seemed sure to come, and moved forward again. The dogs advanced on one another, no longer noticing the camels or the three important men who had come out of the stable and, ignoring the pleading crowd of beggars, were now rummaging in their saddlebags. The camel drivers stood by helpfully, holding things their employers handed to them. But the dogs paid no attention to these goings-on. They had eyes only for each other.

When the three men found the jars and boxes they had been looking for, they solemnly started back to the stable, carrying the objects carefully. Again the beggars crowded around them. On the way the group passed between Lila and the strange dog, who had not stopped his menacing advance. But with people suddenly blocking the view, the dogs couldn't see each other. To Lila, the momentary break in eye contact with the stranger seemed almost as if he had dropped his gaze in a failure of courage. Emboldened, she hurried forward, and when the path cleared, she was startled to find herself face-to-face with him.

His iron stance and hard stare brought her abruptly to a stop. Lila realized that he was the dog of the scent marks, the chief dog of the village. But, up close, he seemed not quite as tough as she had been expecting. For one thing, he wasn't as big as she was. Few dogs were. And he seemed younger than she was, too. Not quite so worried by him, she relaxed a little. He took the moment to advance. Before she knew it, they were side by side, facing past one another, turning to size each other up. She would have switched her hips aside to deny him her hindquarters, but quickly and firmly he pressed his nose down on her shoulder. Under pressure, she stood perfectly still, her eyes wide, her ears half down, leaning away from him with one forefoot raised. Then, ignoring the message of her tucked hips and clamped tail, the bold stranger investigated her thoroughly, learning her sex,

Up close, he seemed not quite as tough as she had been expecting.

her age, the condition of her womb and ovaries, the contents of her stomach and intestines, the amount and type of protein she had eaten recently, her relationship (none) to the dogs of the village, and, as near as he could tell, her place of origin. His head was only a little higher than her shoulder, she noticed, but as he circled her he once again thrust his nose down onto her mantle as if to hold her in place. He seemed to think that he outranked her.

But then, as he turned to face her, halting the interview, she saw that his entire body had gone soft and his eyes had grown alert and tender. He was anxious to know what she thought of him. He wanted her to like him. She saw that he liked her very much.

The stranger was a village dog with a tough if skinny body and strong if skinny legs. His fur was short, his ears were erect, his face was narrow, and his tongue had dark spots on it. His name was Yom, not that Lila ever knew it, since it was merely the name his former owner had called him, probably because of his hazy yellow fur. By the time he met Lila, he had no owner. Something had gone wrong with his owners—he didn't know what. He had come home one day to find the house empty and the family gone. He had waited for them for several days, but when new people came and took the house, they drove him away. So he had gone on to live with the rest of the village dogs, most of whom were also homeless. With them he scavenged for scraps in the gutters, caught a mouse or a rat or a dove now and then, and drank the water that seeped into the muddy footprints of cattle and donkeys near the trough by the fenced-off village spring.

A smell of the alleys clung to his fur, Lila noticed as she looked him over. His forceful walk, raised ears, and bold carriage made him seem sure of himself. From the scars on his ears, neck, and legs, Lila saw that he knew something of fighting, and from his proud bearing she guessed that he had won most of his battles. She wanted to explore further the tender feelings he seemed to have for her and, going down on her elbows, she invited him to play. Then she noticed that they were being approached by a pack of dogs.

These were the village dogs whom Lila had been dreading. They had silently emerged from an alley while she and Yom were absorbed with each other. Gathering her courage, Lila drew herself up to face them. Three males and two females, the strangers looked very much like Yom, with thin bodies, fair hair, curved tails, upright ears, and narrow faces. Heads low, mantles raised, teeth long and white, they glared at Lila savagely. She could see that she was in for a battle that, big as she was, she might not win. She glanced at Yom to see whose side he'd take.

Head and tail high, feet firmly planted, Yom without hesitation placed himself between Lila and the village dogs. If they wanted to fight her, they would fight him too, and fight him first. Lila saw them falter. Evidently Yom hadn't won his scars for nothing. For a moment, everyone waited, motionless. The two females ran their eyes up and down Lila, taking in her long teeth and formidable size. The three males looked at Yom, taking in the fact that he was claiming Lila. Then, with a proud air, feigning calm although the hair along his spine was raised, one of them stepped forward to Lila as if he meant to investigate her as Yom had done. But Yom wheeled about and with a short roar snapped his jaws just in front of the strange male's face. No one but Yom would investigate Lila. The stranger turned his head slightly, lowered his ears, and squinted his eyes. He wasn't going to fight Yom. Pretending a loss of interest, he stepped aside, then stiffly and slowly retreated to a nearby wall which he investigated briefly, and then marked casually, as if any mark he might make in the context of the moment meant little to him. The other two male dogs did the same, then all three took turns slowly, stiffly marking other walls. The tension was diminishing. The two female dogs let Yom touch their noses in greeting, then trotted off with their male companions among the camels in the square. Lila looked at Yom to see if he would stay with her or follow the others. He would stay, she saw to her joy.

. . .

So Yom and Lila played for a moment or two. Then Yom turned and ran, and Lila followed gladly. He led her among the groaning camels to the door of the inn, right where the star odor was strongest. Yom had timed the moment perfectly—they ran up at the very instant the cook tossed out the garbage. Chasing away a rat and some doves, the two dogs quickly dined on sheep gristle and vegetable peelings. Some angels arrived a few moments later, perhaps hoping for a share of the vegetable peelings, but not a scrap remained.

Seven

The kings had come to Bethlehem in response to a prophecy. For their journey they had chosen to provide their own accommodations rather than to rent quarters in the noisy, squalid towns along the way. From his home in Nubia, the white-haired, black-skinned King Melchior had brought tents of heavy silk; from his home in India, the black-haired, brown-skinned King Gaspar had brought rich carpets; and from his home in Tarsis, the brown-haired, white-skinned King Balthazar had brought cooking equipment and bedding. Every night of their journey, their steward would direct the lower-ranking servants to pitch camp in the clean, quiet beauty of the desert.

Understandably, however, making camp with so much

baggage took time, and after the kings had gone into the stable to offer their gifts of gold and precious resins, the steward ordered the other servants to pack up. With him they would go on ahead to pitch the tents, arrange the rugs and bedding, and prepare the evening meal. The kings would follow later and find everything done.

While the camel drivers shouted and the camels roared and groaned, most of the caravan made ready to depart. This time even the serving men mounted, all but one of the drivers, who when everyone else was in a saddle untied the hobbles. Released, the great beasts rose up, hind legs first, while their tilting passengers clung to the harness straps. The driver stood on the folded foreleg of the last camel until the procession was moving, then quickly swung into the saddle as that camel, too, sprang to his feet. Two royal white riding camels were forced to wait to bring the kings later, and they moaned and struggled against their hobbles when they saw that they would be left behind.

Slowly the square emptied, except for the two unhappy camels. Doves flew down to peck at the dung. The caravan squeezed into a narrow track that went west, the direction in which, according to the innkeeper, the travelers would find a stretch of beautiful countryside where there was a spring and a good campsite, out of the wind between two hills.

The innkeeper had also assured King Gaspar's huntsman that because of the spring he would find gazelles and bustards there. King Gaspar liked to do a bit of hunting on his journeys. Whenever possible, he brought his eagle and cheetah. The sport gave him great pleasure, and the public interest aroused by his animals gave him a sense of quiet pride. These emotions were not shared by the animals, though. Imprisoned in their baskets on the last departing camel, they were forced to endure the curious stares of bystanders. The cheetah didn't try to mask her feelings; she cowered behind the wicker with darting, anxious eyes. But the eagle could coldly outstare anyone. The gawkers meant less than nothing to him. Head high, he seemed not even to notice that he wore two leather straps, two shackle-like jesses, on his ankles.

The dogs watched him go. After eating, they were resting together behind the open door of the stable. People and angels were going in and out; when they left, especially if they were moving quickly, they trailed little clouds of air. Testing this air for a better sense of what was happening in the dark interior, Lila's nose told her that two donkeys were present, one a stallion and the other a mare. A cow and her calf were in there too, also a ram, some ewes, a barn owl, a colony of rats that included the rat Yom and Lila had chased from their dinner, and also a colony of mice. There was hay and straw, milk and grain, some things made of leather, lots of different kinds of cloth—the garments of the people—a small amount of water, a woman with milk in her breasts who was still bleeding from having recently given birth, and many men, including those who had come with the camels. Of the latter, Lila tried to detect which were the kings and which the servants. But since she didn't know them by their personal odors, she found that even she needed her eyes to know their rank. The kings looked proud and calm, and the servants looked busy or anxious or humble. And their clothing looked different. But as for their odors, they were all male human beings, who with their food and their cheetah and their frankincense and myrrh had traveled far on camels. Beyond that, she could make no distinction.

But there was much inside the stable that had nothing to do with the kings and their servants. For one thing, the star odor was extremely strong. At first, Lila took it to be wafting from the angels who kept coming and going. She recognized one, the large male angel who had stood between his flock and Lila when they first met each other. Bowing low, Lila greeted this angel, who in turn recognized her and, with a slow and gracious sweep of his arm, invited the two dogs to enter.

Yom and Lila exchanged a glance. Yom seemed uncomfortable. The citizens of Bethlehem didn't think much of stray dogs, and he had been chased from the door of this inn many times before. But Lila saw no harm in accepting the invitation of the angel, so, very cau-

tiously, ready to dodge a kick from one of the human beings or a cut with a stick or a whip, she stepped inside.

Slowly her hair rose and her skin crawled and prickled
as if before a storm. She knew she was in the presence of
extraordinary power; she knew that many important
things were there inside that dark, dusty space that were
not visible. Again there was the star odor, stronger than
ever. It came from the far end of the stable, that pure star
essence of honey and water, of rock and cedar, and
seemed to pour into the air like scent from a newly
opened flower, clear, beautiful, almost dizzying. Very
humble, very alert, Lila kept to the wall and inched toward its source as inconspicuously as possible.

Soon Lila realized that the source was in a manger. A
group of people, mostly kings and pilgrims, knelt around
the manger with their heads bowed, their eyes shut, and
their hands, palms together, under their noses. Lila knew
that they were begging. Dogs, too, bowed humbly when
begging for something. Quietly, Lila crept among them
until she too could see into the manger.

To her surprise, in it was something that looked for all
the world like a human child. It was resting on hay, fast
asleep with its hands curled, just like the infants born to
her master and his wife. But Lila clearly remembered the
scent of those infants—a mixture of faintly sour human
milk and of warm, clean skin—and she immediately understood that the child in the manger was not a human

Quietly, Lila crept among them until she too could see into the manger.

being. Unquestionably it had to do with human beings, and even to Lila it looked very much like one of them. But from the storm power that hung about the manger, from the electric feeling in her skin so strong as to be almost painful, Lila knew that the infant was more closely akin to the angels than to the human beings, and most closely akin to the star.

For a long time Lila looked at the little creature, noticing its lips move and its eyelids flutter as if it dreamed of nursing. Any infant would, she knew, being too young to know of anything else. The sight of it, so delicate and tender, made Lila's heart go soft. And although she was just a dog who could never hope to understand everything, as she looked at the infant she understood one thing very clearly. Despite the mighty storm forces and the overwhelming star odor that surrounded the manger, the creature inside it was helpless.

Why then were the kneeling people begging from it? Lila couldn't tell what they wanted, but they clearly wanted something. Their need made Lila uneasy. She knew that human beings didn't sense most sounds or odors, but they were very quick to sense frailty. This put the little creature in danger. Even if it was not exactly one of them, the human beings should be looking for ways to take care of it, not trying to make it take care of them. It was too young to be put to use.

Her mind's eye saw her own four puppies. She remembered their warm skin, their tightly closed ears and eyes, their tiny puffs of breath. Shortly after their birth she had gone, on her master's orders, to bring in his sheep, trusting her master and his wife to safeguard her puppies as anyone would. But the human beings had not protected them. Inexplicably, they had put her puppies into a deep basin of water. Lila had come home to find their tiny bodies cold and wet and still, scattered on the bare ground outside her master's house. If they had lived, they would be grown by now.

The sleeping infant also reminded Lila of her young sheep, alone and unprotected. Soon the day would end. Lila knew that Ima was wise and brave, but she also knew that a goat could not hold her own against the wolves and wild cats who might visit the vineyard to see what moved there after dark.

Made anxious by the thought of helpless creatures needing care, Lila looked once again at the sleeping infant in the manger. Then she quietly left the stable and went out into the afternoon sun.

Yom greeted her eagerly, but her mind was now very much on her sheep, and instead of frisking with him or dropping to her elbows to invite him to play, she gave him a long, deep look. Please come with me, her eyes said. Then, watching him over her shoulder to see if he would follow, she started walking slowly, head and tail low, toward the far side of the square. Yom hesitated for a moment, casting a glance at the door of the inn from which, later in the day, more scraps could fly.

Lila understood what he was thinking. She too would have liked to stay near a source of food, and she knew of none in the vineyard. If Yom had decided to stay, she would have accepted his decision. But to her joy, he brightened and ran to her side. Lila was so happy with his choice that she went down on her elbows after all. Tenderly, he caught her muzzle in his mouth. For a moment they frisked and then, tails high, they found the track and trotted companionably westward in the swirling cloud of odor shed by the kings' caravan—a heady mixture of camel, man, cat, myrrh, and extraordinary delicacies. Hurried along by Lila's sense of urgency and the spell of the food, the dogs paused only to nose the dung dropped by the camels or to investigate the marks of other dogs.

Eight

Under the spreading olive tree at the edge of the vineyard, Ima and the sheep chewed their cuds. Feeling much better, the angel dozed for a while, her head on Ima's flank. She then groomed the young sheep, scratching behind their ears and along the sides of their noses. The sheep loved that and pushed one another to get near her. But the shadows were getting long, and Ima felt uneasy. She didn't want to spend the night without Lila. Swallowing her cud before it was ready, while it still had coarse stems and bark from the grapevines in it, she got to her feet to look for the dog.

When she stood up, the others got up too. The young sheep spread out to browse, and the angel crouched down to look for raisins under the grapevines. Ima didn't want the youngsters to know that she was getting anxious. She was just considering whether to climb the tree again when she heard a rush of wings. Hoping that perhaps someone had come to find the young angel, she looked up and saw not an angel but an eagle. Leather thongs trailed strangely from his ankles, giving him a bizarre appearance—a great, dangerous, free-flying creature who wore fetters. The sheep looked up too, puzzled by the queer sight.

Then the eagle sailed right over them. Ima became alarmed. Years before, while shepherding with Lila, she had seen what the young sheep had not, an eagle stooping on a lamb, snatching the helpless infant from his mother's side and carrying him into the sky, with nothing that Ima or Lila or the mother ewe could do about it. Noting that all the birds in the vineyard had fallen silent, Ima realized that this slowly wheeling eagle was studying her and her charges. She tossed her horns at the eagle, showing how she would toss him if he came any nearer. But the eagle had no further interest in her or the sheep— he was looking for something large with feathers that would please both himself and his falconer—so he tilted his wings and circled away, his jesses trailing.

The sheep returned to their food. But Ima didn't like the look of the eagle, and she kept her eye on his slow turn. She glanced from him to her sheep to the angel, and suddenly a terrifying thought struck her. With a loud cry of warning, she ran bucking toward the angel, giving her a nasty scare. But Ima had read the eagle's mind. The angel looked up just in time to see the huge eagle, his talons outstretched, plummeting down on her out of the sun. Just before he struck she leaped out of the way, upsetting his balance.

From the moment when, high in the air, the eagle had folded his wings and plunged down to the feathered creature below, he had expected to sink his talons into a large bird. When, instead of a bird, an angel suddenly stood up in front of him, the eagle was astonished. The shock almost knocked him out of the air. But he nevertheless managed to land on his feet, even though he had to rock back and forth, balancing with his wings and tail to collect himself. He and the angel looked at each other.

The eagle was huge. His head came almost to the angel's waist. He was also a little angry, as if the angel had fooled him. With every bit of his customary skill, he had stooped on a bird, only to see at the last possible instant that it wasn't a bird at all. The eagle didn't like surprises, and he glared at the angel.

The angel was a little angry too. There she was peacefully looking for raisins when this great dragon plunged on her from the sky. One of the laws of nature says that birds don't prey on angels and angels don't prey on birds, mostly because both are of the air and thus are related to each other. The young she-angel had never heard of a bird attacking one of her kind. Eagle and angel exchanged disapproving stares.

But if the eagle was sorry, he didn't let on. Hawks and eagles never apologize or show remorse for their errors—they don't even blink their yellow eyes. To seem insensitive is just their custom, the way they are. But that doesn't mean they don't know when they're wrong. The eagle knew. With a last look at the angel he turned aside so that he wouldn't take off right over her—a courtesy of sorts—then he spread his strong wings, leaned forward, ran a step or two flapping, and majestically lifted his huge body into the air. With flawless dignity he circled, gaining altitude, then flew away to the south. And that was that. Compared to the ignominy of his trailing jesses, ignominy he overcame without effort, a slip of the kind he had just experienced seemed not to matter at all.

Ima expected no reward or gratitude for her helpful but very natural act; she was just glad that no damage had been done and that the eagle was leaving. She was therefore very touched when the angel knelt beside her and embraced her. It wasn't what a goat would do—in a similar situation, goats would rub faces—but it was thoughtful just the same. Pleased with the gesture even though it made her feel a little shy, Ima shook her tail.

When the eagle was the size of a fly in the distance, the young angel also took to the air and flew away to the east, the direction Lila had taken that morning. Perhaps the angel would see Lila, Ima thought. Perhaps Lila would see the angel and remember that she was needed by those she'd left behind. Creatures far more dangerous than eagles could visit the vineyard at night.

But perhaps something had happened to Lila, or perhaps she had changed her mind about protecting Ima and the sheep. She was a dog, after all, not a goat. And then, as Ima always did when feeling distressed, she pictured the fold where she was born, remembering how her relatives would keep together. And she wished very much that they were with her there in the vineyard. If they were, they would protect her. They would all protect one another. That was how it was with goats.

However, Ima knew that no good ever came from thinking frightening thoughts or from wanting what you cannot have. With a shake of her tail she composed herself, and was about to put her head into one of the vines for a few more mouthfuls when suddenly something happened that frightened her far more than the eagle had. A young gazelle with foaming mouth and bulging eyes burst out of the brush and tore across the vineyard just ahead of a huge, thin, long-legged cat, who, eyes wide and tail aloft, was rapidly closing on him. For an instant, Ima and the sheep stared in horror, then they leaped away in all directions as the gazelle suddenly veered and ran straight for them. He passed among them like a blast of wind, almost knocking them over, and the next thing Ima knew, a struggling sheep was down on the ground and the huge

*A young gazelle burst out of the brush and tore across the vineyard
just ahead of a huge, thin, long-legged cat.*

cat was on top of her, choking her with a bite to the throat.

Gasping for breath, the gazelle slowed, then turned to look back. Realizing that as far as he was concerned the danger was over, he trotted away among the olive trees at the far end of the vineyard.

What could be done? Ima and the surviving sheep could only stand by in helpless dismay as the downed sheep's struggle ended. The cheetah no longer seemed dangerous—indeed, she seemed hardly to know they were there. Without giving them so much as a glance, she sighed deeply and raised her bloodstained face to look back in the direction from which she had come. Ima followed her gaze and saw a cloud of dust, and inside it a white camel. On the camel rode two men, King Gaspar and his huntsman, both looking worried, both trying hard to make the camel trot.

The cheetah moved down a row of vines and began to wash her face. Afraid of the camel, Ima and the sheep crept slowly toward the edge of the vineyard, not daring to run for fear of tempting the cheetah into chasing them. When the two men found the cheetah they made the camel kneel and slid off her back. Then they saw the murdered sheep and shouted many loud and angry words at the cheetah. These the cheetah ignored, and calmly went on washing herself. What was the use of trying to inspire guilt in a cat?

The two men looked around in all directions, calling,

trying to find the shepherd who owned the sheep. The huntsman even took out a ram's horn and blew a loud blast. But when no one appeared, the king swung the carcass over the saddle and then climbed up himself. His huntsman tied one end of a rope to the camel's harness and the other end to the cheetah's collar and, allowing the cheetah plenty of slack, hauled himself up behind his master. The men shouted at the camel, who unbent her hind legs, then her front legs, and struck out for the kings' camp. Not until the rope stretched tight would the cheetah get up and follow. The camel wasn't happy that a large cat was close behind her, and the cheetah wasn't happy to be near such a dangerous pair of heels, but what could either animal do? Making the best of the bad situation, they trudged along with lowered heads and flattened ears and soon were out of sight.

Nine

Trotting purposefully, Yom and Lila made their way west along the dusty track. Ahead of them the sun slipped behind the hills. Feeling her hair tickle gently with the power of the star, Lila looked back over her shoulder at the eastern horizon. There the new star—which on that night was the first star—was slowly beginning to show itself in the darkening sky. Thinking very much of Ima and the sheep, Lila picked up her pace a little. The darker it got, the more she worried.

Yom trotted behind. He assumed that Lila was following the camels, and was therefore surprised when she suddenly turned north and headed into the bush. But as she gave every sign of knowing what she was doing, he gave a mental shrug and went along.

Weaving through the thornbushes and palmettos, the dogs came at last to the vineyard. There Lila stopped to look around. Yom looked too and saw, behind a screen of thornbush at the edge of the vineyard, a flock of sheep and a goat at rest, slowly chewing. Joy! There seemed to be no shepherd with them, and no dog! With a cry of pleasure, he threw himself toward them and was gaining speed when he heard a great roar and fell sideways. Lila had smashed into him. Astonished, he looked at her for an explanation, but she was advancing toward the flock.

At the approach of the dogs, the sheep got up, gulped their cuds, and, wary, moved deeper into the bushes. Only the goat came forward. Lila was puzzled by the shyness of the sheep, but, head low and tail waving, she went forward happily to greet Ima. Ima stood stiffly, allowing Lila to sniff her mouth and shoulders. She did not respond when Lila then dropped briefly to her elbows as if asking her to play, but Lila hadn't really expected the goat to frolic with her. She had only wanted to signal her joy. As she moved off to inspect the sheep, the goat stayed close to her side.

The sheep seemed torn between caution and relief. Slowly they began to edge back toward their shepherds. Yom saw that this place was where Lila belonged. Here he, not she, was the stranger. Respectfully, he held back as Lila examined the sheep, sniffing their feet, their rumps, their mouths, their shoulders, just as if they were other dogs.

Suddenly Lila gave a cough of dismay. The hair on her shoulders rose. Nose to the earth, she began to hurry back and forth. Without really knowing what he was looking for, Yom joined the search. In a moment his hair, too, rose like Lila's. He had found the scents of death, of fear, of blood, and of a ewe he hadn't known. Bits of her wool were still tangled in the grapevines. He also found the scents of a female camel, a female cheetah, and two male human beings, and he knew he had seen them all in front of the inn.

That night the animals slept poorly or not at all. The sheep wouldn't lie down but stood bunched together, calling to one another from time to time, perhaps for reassurance that the others were still there. Ima lay apart from them but kept her eyes open. Lila lay down for a while next to Yom but, overcome by a sense of unrest, got up again and went to the place where the sheep had been killed, where the earth was still soaked with the smells of fear and death, of blood and cheetah. Again Lila nosed the bits of wool tangled in the vines and saw the sheep's face in her mind's eye. She nosed the path where the sheep, the men, and the cheetah had all been carried away by the camel, the camel's odor still atop her footprints, the odors of those she carried spread over the vines on either side. Could Lila have prevented this? She knew she would have tried.

The crescent moon hung in the west, reminding Lila of the high pastures where their journey began. She remembered her doomed infants. She remembered the helpless infant in the manger. And she shivered at the terrible things that lie in wait for helpless creatures whom no one will defend. Lila lifted her head and howled, her voice rising, then falling. When she finished, she found Yom beside her, looking at her intently. So she raised her head a second time and he raised his, and they both howled, as do dogs who have much in their hearts.

Ten

At the royal camp, dawn found the huntsman and the falconer hard at work by firelight, readying the king's animals for another day of sport. It was their custom to hunt with the cheetah at dawn and dusk when antelope were most active, and to hunt with the eagle toward the middle of the day when birds were most active. That morning they were taking two camels—a white riding camel for King Gaspar and a large brown working camel for the falconer, the huntsman, the eagle, and, despite her crimes of the day before, the cheetah. Disappointed by the cheetah's misbehavior, the huntsman wanted to give her more practice with the right kind of quarry. He hoped that a chance to chase an-

*Dawn found the huntsman and the falconer hard at work by firelight,
readying the king's animals for another day of sport.*

other gazelle would straighten her out. A servant had packed saddlebags with cooked food and jars of wine and water—the party would hunt all day.

King Gaspar let the servants make the preparations. He was busy that morning, as he had been every morning since the star had first appeared, with the brown-haired King Balthazar, who had taken out his Greek astrolabe, and with the white-haired King Melchior, who had unrolled his maps of the zodiac. With this equipment plus Gaspar's own astrological charts, the royal men studied the new star in the hour before dawn. But when the sky began to pale, Gaspar abandoned the study to his companions and, vaulting into his saddle, urged his white camel to her feet. Then, with the larger, more heavily burdened camel trying to keep up with him, he led his party north.

Not a hundred paces from the camp the white camel flushed a gazelle, a strong young male with a fine pair of horns, who sprang from the clump of bushes he had been browsing and raced away to the west. Instantly the huntsman slid down over the rump of the second camel and released the cheetah, who needed a moment to spot what it was she was supposed to be chasing, and then sped off in pursuit. The gazelle stopped to look back, trying to evaluate the danger, but when he saw that a cheetah was rapidly gaining on him he went bounding off again.

The gazelle was in the prime of life and almost as fast as the cheetah. Also, he had been chased before by wolves and he knew how to zigzag confusingly. When the cheetah got near him he did just that, throwing her off for a moment. And in that moment the cheetah remembered how simple it had been to kill a sheep. All she had needed to do was to knock it down and bite its throat. No chasing, no breathlessness, no pounding heart. Without further ado she turned her rump to the gazelle and his fancy sidestepping and leaped away through the brush in the direction of the vineyard. When the huntsman saw what she was doing, he cursed her for a bad and willful cat and blew a commanding blast on his horn, but the cheetah hardly heard him. She was out of sight before the camels could even get turned around.

Stuck with grass seeds and in a cloud of dust, the king and his party arrived at the vineyard sure that they would find a few dead sheep, but not at all sure that they would find their cheetah. What they saw amazed them. The sheep were all alive and well, all standing around as if something had just happened. But the cheetah had been taken prisoner.

She lay as if toppled, rolled almost on her back, displaying most of her white belly. Over her stood a huge gray dog, holding her down with a threatening face, bared teeth, and staring eyes. Ears back and wrist limp, the cheetah seemed the very picture of submission. Even so, her twitching tail spoke of her displeasure, and her steady hissing called attention to her sharp white teeth, which showed, she hoped, how dangerous she could be when necessary. The dog was not impressed.

The king was, though. He and his huntsman looked at the dog with admiration. No man had been able do much with this cheetah, and suddenly here was a dog who had brought her under control—and before, not after, she'd done something dreadful.

As the camels approached, the dog drew back. Thus released, the cheetah twisted to a sitting position as if to run, but she spotted the huntsman sliding from the saddle and, relieved that he had come to her rescue, allowed him to slip the rope under her collar. Although he was still cross with her, he scratched her head grudgingly when she rubbed him with her face. Leaving the future entirely to him, she flopped herself down in the shade of the camel.

The king dismounted and began to speak in excited tones to the huntsman while glancing at the big dog. They were talking about her, Lila knew. Furtive behavior troubles a dog as it troubles any animal, so Lila kept her distance. Still, she always thought it better to keep an eye on any creature who appeared to be up to no good, so she watched the men warily. She saw the huntsman rummage briefly in a saddlebag and produce a rope. She saw the huntsman whirl the rope around his head, but the gesture made no sense to her. Then suddenly she was noosed and choking.

The day was getting warmer. Bustards would be searching through the grass for locusts. As the falconer put it to the king, it was time to loose the eagle. Stuffing the unwilling cheetah back into her basket, the men remounted and goaded the camels, who stood up reluctantly and moved forward. The hunting party left the vineyard with the king in solitary dignity atop the royal riding camel and the huntsman, the falconer, the eagle, the cheetah, and the saddlebags all somehow fastened to the larger, working camel, who now had to drag a dog as well.

Deeply distressed by what was happening, and alarmed at the prospect of staying any longer in this dangerous land without protection, Ima followed Lila. Although Lila didn't look much like a guardian at that moment—dragged along helplessly in a cloud of dust kicked up by a camel—she was all that Ima had. The sheep never questioned what to do. They followed their two shepherds.

Yom also followed. He had been standing by, dismayed at Lila's struggles but powerless to help her. He was frightened by the noise, the dust, the camels, and the men, but he knew that wherever they were taking Lila, he'd have to follow. Giving himself a shake to throw off a foreboding of great danger, he trotted behind the camels at a distance. He found the scent of fear in every one of Lila's sweaty footprints, and the hair along his backbone rose.

• • •

When the hunting party reached the brushy countryside where bustards might be found, the men were irritated to see that the goat and flock of sheep had somehow followed them. But when the falconer stopped the camels to release the eagle, the sheep spread out to graze, and the king and his huntsmen forgot about them. In this pastoral country, they realized, sheep were never far away. Quietly, so as not to alarm potential quarry, the falconer brought the eagle to his wrist.

But Ima had had enough of this eagle. At the sight of his enormous body so close by, she bleated a warning. She had meant to warn the sheep, but all the animals in the area heard her, including a pair of bustards in the distance. Alarmed, they flapped into the air and out of sight. The hunt was spoiled.

Furious, the huntsman picked up a stone and flung it at Ima. It hit her horn, almost stunning her. Hurt and startled, she ran bucking among the sheep, panicking them and sending them dashing in all directions. The sudden rush of unruly sheep scattering under and around them caused the camels to rear. They didn't know what was wrong, but if others were escaping, then they also wanted to escape, and without riders to hinder them. Helpless to control the sheep or, for that matter, the camels, Lila howled dismally. Yom threw back his head and joined his voice to hers. The eagle quickly had his fill of the confusion and, despite his hood, launched himself into the air. But the falconer was holding his jesses, and immediately the eagle found himself hanging head down. Eagles are so dignified that they cannot be humiliated, even in an awkward position. Wings spread but motionless, the eagle merely dangled, waiting. When the falconer offered him a wrist to stand on, he righted himself with perfect aplomb, then settled his feathers as if nothing had gone wrong. Not so Gaspar, who cursed his white camel for trying to throw him and called off the hunt.

Regaining his composure, the king looked around him. Providence had deprived him of a gazelle and a bustard, so he and his company would have no game for their dinner. But here was a flock of sheep without an owner, sheep who obviously had been destroying someone's vineyard. The vines would be ruined and wolves would eat the sheep. What good would that do anybody? Ordering his huntsman and falconer to round up the sheep and follow, King Gaspar led the party back to camp.

Eleven

*C*hoked by the rope around her neck, Lila wondered desperately where the camel was dragging her. Then, as if her troubled mind were playing tricks on her in her confusion, she noticed the smell of freshly cooked food. The farther the camel dragged her, the stronger grew the scent, and when suddenly the camel stopped and Lila was allowed to stand still, the scent became overpowering. She realized that its source was near.

The kings' camp was fenced with cut thorn branches to discourage wild animals. Because of the fence Lila couldn't see the food or even the kitchen until the camel dragged her through the thornbush gate. Then Lila saw that the heady odor came most strongly from a tent. Even the human beings seemed aware of this ocean of fragrance—King Gaspar slid off his camel and hurried into the tent, followed by his huntsman and falconer. Servants arrived to take away the cheetah, the eagle, and the camels. Other servants came with shepherds' crooks to herd the flock of sheep. Someone tied Lila to a gatepost and left her alone.

She was very uncomfortable. The rope around her neck was too tight and she was too near the gatepost, so that every person or animal who went through the gate came too close to her. She lifted her lip at them but didn't dare growl. Worst of all, in the distance she saw that Ima and the sheep were being guarded by a servant who had assumed the familiar, possessive attitude of a human shepherd leaning on his crook. Meanwhile other servants cut thorn branches and laid them in a semicircle by the camp fence—Lila realized that they were making a pen. The sheep knew nothing of what might be in store for them—they were so young and inexperienced that they didn't even know what a pen was, let alone fear it. They grazed as usual, sensing nothing wrong. But Ima saw the trouble. She didn't graze but watched Lila anxiously, just as Lila was watching her.

Just then, however, something happened that Lila would remember for the rest of her life, something so marvelous and astonishing that she forgot all her fears. Around the corner came the kings' steward carrying a huge brass platter heaped with food. Eyes big with long-ing, Lila swallowed hard, expecting the steward to pass by her on his way somewhere else with this wonderful bounty. But to her amazement, the steward put the plat-ter down in front of her.

Lila had never seen anything like it. Swimming in oil were scraps of mutton, crusts of oatmeal bread, scrapings of barley porridge, wilted vine leaves, and the heads, feet, and wings of many cooked doves. From the pile rose the odor of plenty, the fragrance of kings, so strong that Lila's head spun.

She looked up at the steward, not quite believing that such a prize could be for her. But she saw that the steward was looking at her amiably, waiting for her to begin. Lila started to tremble. An unimaginable feast had been placed in front of her, and she, she of all the dogs in the world, was being invited to eat it. She was being offered more life and strength than she had ever before seen. Such was the power of the human beings. She plunged at the food, bolting as fast as she could.

Suddenly Yom was in front of her, his face almost touching hers. With his nose right above the food, he was looking straight at her, asking for a share. She growled and kept eating, fixing him with a threatening stare. Holding her eyes, he moved his nose a little closer to the food. She could see that he was very hungry. But she was hungry too, and bigger than he was. She needed more food. His nose came even nearer. This was the moment for Lila to roar and bite at him if she was going to—if he got any closer to the platter, he'd be eating. She gathered herself to drive him off.

Just then his gaze faltered. She saw his confidence weaken. A dog like Yom would not hesitate to fight for food, but it seemed he was not going to fight Lila. He recognized the platter as hers by right. And although food is life—and although hunger, sooner or later, is death—he would wait to see which she would choose for him. Lila swallowed hard, remembering how, the day before, Yom had so willingly led her to the innkeeper's scraps. Neither dog had eaten since. Suddenly she dropped her eyes and moved to make a space for him, and in the next instant both were gulping.

Just a few seconds later Yom gave a loud, choked scream and leaped away. Lila looked up, confused and frightened. The steward had kicked him.

Perhaps she had been mistaken. Perhaps the food was not meant for her after all. But the steward again gave Lila an encouraging look. He wanted her to eat. She had become a king's dog and would be fed royal leavings. The steward had only meant that Yom was not to eat. A worthless stray, he was nothing and would be given nothing. Yom limped into the long grass at the edge of camp, and the steward, satisfied that the stray had been driven off, returned to his duties.

Lila again began to eat, not quite as greedily as before.

She tried hard to wait for Yom's return, and although she couldn't keep herself from gulping a few bites, she managed to eat slowly enough so that some food was left when he silently limped back to the remains of the feast. Before the steward could come back to drive Yom away again, the dogs had cleaned the platter with their tongues.

As Lila and Yom were nosing around the edges of the platter in case some tasty scraps had fallen unnoticed to the ground, the servants finished fencing the pen and herded Ima and the sheep inside it. Anxious at being driven into this cramped, unfamiliar place, the sheep took fright, and when the gate was closed and they were shut inside, they began to dash about, bleating in panic. To Lila, dizzy from the feast as her body tried to absorb the shock of so much rich food, the panic of the sheep was terrible. She jumped up instantly, forgetting that she couldn't get to them. The rope snapped her back to earth.

This was terrible. Panic was exactly what sheep were not supposed to do, exactly why they needed a sheepdog to guide and protect them. Their dangerous behavior should be stopped at once, before they bolted or hurt themselves. In great distress, Lila strained at her rope collar, hearing her sheep bolt this way and that, smelling the cloud of their fear. Sometimes she'd sit down briefly, but she was too nervous to sit for long. Often she'd bark with agitation. Once she barked as a servant was passing. He thought she was barking at him and he kicked her. Bravely, Yom snapped at him.

After dark the two exhausted dogs lay down as far from the gatepost as Lila's rope allowed, and slept fitfully. But from time to time they dreamed—from time to time the splendid feast appeared again before them, and again they gulped it to the last delicious morsel. And in the dream, Yom was as welcome as Lila.

Toward morning Lila felt something tickling behind her ear. She woke with a start and saw Ima's slit goat eyes not inches from her own. Ima had escaped from the pen and was chewing Lila's rope collar.

Methodically, Ima munched. It was all Lila could do to keep still because she could hear the sheep escaping from the pen through a widening hole in the fence that surely had been started by Ima. If it hurt Lila to think of the sheep imprisoned, it hurt her even more to think that they were scattering over the countryside, running everywhere, anywhere, out of control. Deeply distressed, she whined and pawed the earth. But Ima could not chew any faster. Not until the sky in the east turned faintly gray did she manage to chew all the way through the collar. Suddenly Lila felt no pressure on her neck and knew she was free.

Lila lowered her ears and looked gratefully at Ima.

They knew they had to go home. Raising her head, Lila tested the air for the scent of her scattered sheep so she would know where to start her roundup. Then she noticed that Ima was looking at the star.

As on the day the two shepherds had first seen it, the star was almost invisible in the gathering dawn. But this morning they noticed that their hair wasn't lifting as if before a storm, and although Lila sniffed and Ima raised her lip to test the air, neither shepherd could find even a trace of the star odor.

So they knew the star was leaving. It seemed to have done what it had come to do and now was withdrawing to its home in the mysterious sky. It reminded Lila of her master, who came before dawn to the high pasture with her ration of food, then turned his back and went away again, leaving the animals alone.

Against the dawn sky the two shepherds noticed a flock of angels flying toward them. At first the angels were all bunched together, but as the two shepherds watched, the flock strung out in a line behind the biggest angels so that the air disturbed by the stronger ones could help lift the weaker ones. They flew vigorously, as if they had not been flying far or for any length of time—they must have left Bethlehem when the first milky light began to show. As the flock came near, the shepherds recognized the angels they had met at the start of the journey. Like the star, the angels would have done whatever they had come to do in Bethlehem and, like the star, they would be returning to their place.

The two shepherds sighed, perhaps a little envious of the angels, who were high in the air, out of reach of King Gaspar's servants, kin to his eagle, faster than his cheetah, on their way home together, their work done. Lila and Ima looked at each other to rid themselves of a frightened, lonely feeling. Their group was not safe. Their work was not done.

But no good could come from such thinking. The group was in danger and the shepherds must hurry. Helped by Yom, who had quickly grasped the principles of herding, Lila bounded away into the shadows, finding one sheep after another and driving them back to Ima. Breathless from running, she would stop from time to time to poke her nose at one or another of the sheep. She couldn't count beyond three or four, but she knew each sheep personally. She knew whom she'd already found and who was still missing. When she would fail to find a certain sheep within the group, she'd run off again. Finally she found the last sheep, hiding in a thicket and very glad to see her. But just as she was driving this sheep toward the others, she heard a despairing cry.

Alarmed, Lila stopped in her tracks, her head raised. She and Yom exchanged a glance. Something was happening to Ima. Letting the last sheep run on by himself to join the flock, which now was in sight, the two dogs raced toward the sound.

• • •

Wh(W)hile Lila and Yom were rounding up the sheep, the cook and his young helper had started to make breakfast. But because King Gaspar's hunt had not been successful, the cook had no meat. So he sent his helper to the new thornbush pen to kill one of the sheep. Moments later, however, the young man ran back in distress to report a gap in the fence and all the sheep missing. The cook cursed and rummaged through his baskets for a rope, which he thrust at his helper, ordering him to search the bushes until he found a sheep. The young man touched his forehead respectfully and hurried to obey.

On the hillside west of camp he spotted the dark shapes of the escaped sheep gathered around the goat. Each animal was looking warily in a different direction, and the young man realized that catching a sheep from this flock would not be easy. Quietly backing away, he found two large stones, tied one to each end of the cook's rope, and began to stalk his quarry. At just the right distance he stopped, whirled the rope around his head, and let go. At the whisper of the stones in the air, Ima and the sheep looked up in alarm, but too late—the rope wrapped itself around Ima.

Instantly the sheep scattered. Instantly the young man ran forward, not at all sorry that his rope had caught the goat instead of one of the sheep. Goat meat is just as tasty as lamb or mutton, and the sheep would be much easier to handle later on, without their clever guardian to do their thinking for them. Grabbing Ima by the horns, the young man dragged her back to camp.

Ima was terrified. She braced her legs and resisted with all the strength in her body, twisting and bucking every step of the way. The steward and the cook were waiting outside the fence with a sharp knife and a bowl to help the young man kill his victim, and the fight Ima put up amused them. They laughed at the young man's difficulty, embarrassing him. Ima's struggles were making a fool of him. He gave her a shake as if to ask for her cooperation.

But Ima fought on because she knew what was happening. She had glimpsed the knife and the bowl. She had seen sheep slaughtered by her master, and she knew what these men meant to do to her. Moments earlier she had been gathering her flock for their homeward journey. Instead, in spite of all her skill and knowledge, she would die in the dirt at the hands of strangers. Her life's blood would run into the bowl, and her body would become meat.

The young man finally managed to wrestle Ima to the ground. He knelt on her to keep her down, holding her by the horn with one hand as he reached for the knife. At that instant, she gave a loud cry of despair.

The cry echoed. Far away, Yom and Lila heard it and they ran toward the sound. On the far side of camp, the cheetah heard it, pricked up her ears, and sprang to the top

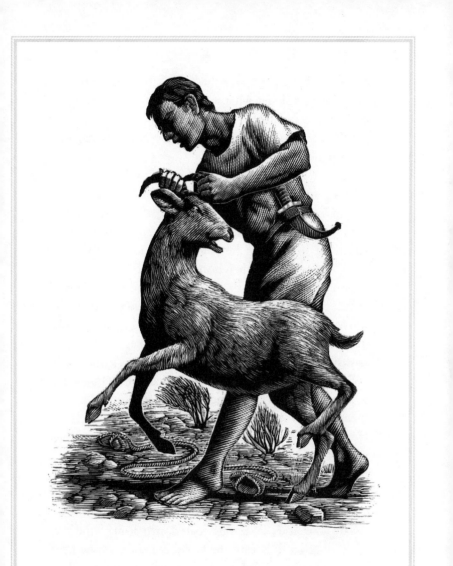

She braced her legs and resisted with all the strength in her body.

of her basket to see over the fence. In their tents, the kings heard it, knew what it meant, and nodded approvingly. The cook and the steward couldn't help but hear it, but they only shrugged their shoulders. Animals about to die commonly scream.

But something in the scream ringing in the ears of the cook's young assistant disturbed him. As he prepared to cut Ima's throat he had been thinking of the meat, wondering how much of a share would be given to the servants. At her scream he paused and noticed that her heart was pounding. He felt the quick rise and fall of her breathing. He noticed that under his hand her horn was warm. Even her horns were alive. And he saw that she was looking at him, looking into his eyes, begging him as in terrible distress one living thing may beg another. He saw that she was begging for her life.

Suddenly he understood. She wanted to live. It seemed so simple. The lives of domestic animals belonged not to them but to their masters. Yet this goat had no master. How easy it would be to do what she so desperately wanted him to do, to give her back her life. He needed only to release her horn and shift his weight from her body. And he did. Ima leaped to her feet and made a dash for freedom.

The cook and the steward roared with dismay, and the cook lunged at Ima with the knife. But suddenly he flew backwards and landed on the ground with a force that left him gasping. A large, dark animal with long white

teeth had pinned him with her forefeet. It was Lila, o
course, and not a moment too soon—Lila with her hair
on end to make herself look big and dangerous even
though she was already big and dangerous!

The cook had not expected such a thing. Aware that
he still held the knife, he angrily slashed at Lila. But his
arm was instantly caught and held motionless—Yom had
seized his wrist. Of course the steward tore a stick from
the fence to beat the dogs away from the cook. But by
now the dogs were making their own dash for freedom,
with Ima up ahead calling all the sheep to follow her and
Lila looking over her shoulder to be sure that Yom was
still there.

Soon Lila and Yom were racing from sheep to sheep,
nipping and barking, keeping them close behind Ima as
she galloped for the high ground. The men had no hope
of overtaking them. Those who witnessed the escape
shrugged their shoulders, disappointed to see such a valuable dog and so much lamb and mutton vanishing into
the bush. Only the huntsman had an inspiration.

All this time the cheetah had been sitting high atop
her basket, craning her neck to see over the fence. She
had held her breath with excitement as the goat escaped,
and again as the dogs escaped. By the time the huntsman
came to loose her tether, she was taut with energy, and
she rubbed him with her face. Pleased, he gave her an af-
fectionate pat and pointed to the vanishing Lila. But as
any cat might, the cheetah misinterpreted the hunts-

man's signal. The moment she felt her tether drop she sped away to her own freedom, and not in the direction of the formidable Lila. No creature on earth could have caught her.

Once the shepherds and their flock had reached the high ground, Lila tested the wind as she always did in a new place to learn what was around her, and she noticed a familiar odor. It was the perfume of the kings' food, their breakfast, which had been cooking unsupervised during all the excitement. Now this scent of life, of strength, came wafting up the hillside on the east wind, and Lila couldn't help but stop to savor it. Looking back, she saw the kings' camp spread out below—a tableau of royal life, of comfort, ease, and glorious food—a life that could have been hers. But Yom had not been welcome there. And Ima and the sheep had been in danger. Yom would have been stoned and driven away and, one by one, Ima and the sheep would have furnished those mouthwatering royal meals.

And if the king's camp was not a place for them, it was therefore not a place for Lila. She was a shepherd. Her place was with those who were in her care, and her task was to protect them. She knew her duty. And all she wanted was to do her duty—nothing less or more. Turning from her vision of the kings and their food, she raced after the sheep, urging them to hurry.

Twelve

With the sheep in their orderly flock behind Ima, and with Lila and Yom in the rear, alert for lagging or danger, the animals went home. Ima and Lila set the pace at a purposeful trot, not making the sheep travel too fast but not letting them linger, either. And the shepherds didn't need a star or anything else to guide them. Capable animals always know what route will bring them home.

The fourth evening found them in the harvested wheat field where they had met the angels at the very start of their journey. Near the oak with its abundant supply of acorns they found the angels again, sheltered from the wind by a hedge of cedar shrubs, sitting around some little fires. They didn't appear to be in any hurry. At one of the fires was Ima's friend, the young she-angel, who greeted her affectionately.

It would have been pleasant to spend some time with these angels enjoying the warmth of the fires on such a cold night. But the hour was late, and the tired young sheep would be apt to stray. Lila and Ima exchanged a glance, and in the eyes of the other, each shepherd saw her own thought: they had best move on. So with Yom's help Lila gathered the sheep into a neat flock that moved smartly along behind Ima, and they went on to their master's stable. The door was shut, but they lay down and slept outside.

The master and his wife were already in bed and didn't hear the animals, but when they woke in the morning they praised their maker that the livestock had returned. They didn't seem to mind that one sheep was missing—this was the sheep who had been killed by the cheetah—either because they didn't notice or because they were so glad to see the rest. For the safe return of their flock they credited Lila. They even praised and thanked her. Their pleasure made her very happy. Giving little cries of joy, she wagged her tail and with it the entire rear of her body as she kissed their hands.

The master and his wife were surprised to see Yom, but in those days a stray dog meant less than nothing as long as he didn't kill sheep. And although the master and his wife, being human, noticed very little, they couldn't help but notice that the sheep were not afraid of Yom but

stayed close to him trustfully. Danger to sheep was all
that concerned the two people. They shrugged and forgot
their concerns about Yom.

Before taking the sheep to their pasture, the master fed
Lila from a basin containing barley gruel and a few table
scraps. Very hungry from the long trip with so little to
eat, she plunged her head into the basin and would have
bolted the food all by herself, but Yom stood by so
bravely, looking at her hopefully but not begging or trying to force her, that she made room for his head too. Of
course, the master tried to drive him off, just as the kings'
steward had done, but Lila stood up tall and looked so
boldly and directly at her master that a little shiver
passed through him, giving him second thoughts, and he
went back to his house for a splash of milk and some
bread crusts. So both dogs ate something.

Later that morning the master whistled for Lila to
round up the sheep, and he led them all to a familiar upland pasture. There they stayed, living the life that Lila
and Ima had grown used to and Yom soon came to know,
a life of cold winter nights and warm summer days filled
with the smell of cedar.

Ima continued to dream of her experience with the
cook's helper, feeling his great weight on her body and his
powerful hand on her horn, twisting her head. She would
wake in terror and have to stand up and shake herself to

get rid of the dream. For reassurance she would look at Lila in the moonlight or starlight, perhaps hoping that Lila would wake up to keep her company for a little while. But ever since Lila had found Yom she slept very soundly, curled at his side. So Ima would chew her cud for a while, wishing that she could live with other goats as she once had lived with her mother and her father, with her aunts and cousins and brothers and sisters in the fold where she was born.

Then one fine day in early fall, when the sheep and their shepherds were resting together on the windswept slope of a high pasture, they heard the voice of goat on the ridge above. At the same time they noticed on the wind a cloud of star fragrance mixed with goat odor. They all looked up. Sure enough, there stood a young she-angel and a huge male goat.

Immediately the animals recognized the angel as she who had fed them acorns, whom Ima had cured with a spiny plant. But the goat was a stranger. He seemed to have come from the wild hills like a bandit king. His shoulders were massive, his beard was black, his splendid horns made scythelike silhouettes against the sun. And guided by the angel's pointing finger, his blazing, golden eyes had spotted Ima.

He called a second time, louder than before. Ima was paying close attention. Hastily swallowing her cud, she stared directly at him but kept perfectly still. The angel gave him an encouraging nudge. He called again.

Hind legs first, Ima stood up and shook her tail. Still looking at the huge goat, she thought for a moment and at last answered him lightly. *Maa-a-a-ah!*

His glad response echoed from the hills and the valleys. Then suddenly Ima was hurrying toward him. Up the hillside she ran, rattling the stones. In moments she was beside him. He raised his upper lip as she approached, and when she reached him they touched noses.

Ima didn't stop there, however. Instead, trotting past the huge goat, she kept right on going. Abruptly he wheeled and followed her. Lila watched them climb the ridge, Ima slightly in the lead. Next to the giant, she seemed small and rather dainty. Next to her, he seemed huge and almost frightening. Lila thought that Ima might look back at the rest of them, a gesture of farewell, but no—Ima's eyes were on the future. She didn't even look back for the big male. She didn't need to. She could hear his footsteps close behind her and feel his breath on her flank.

The young she-angel watched them go. Then she ran a few steps, rose flapping into the air, circled once to get her bearings, and flew up into the firmament. The two goats climbed to the skyline and vanished over the ridge. Lila never saw them again.

After that, an old ewe took Ima's place as teacher of the young sheep. She was not as wise as Ima and not as

The two goats climbed to the skyline and vanished over the ridge.

friendly with the dogs, because after all she was a sheep and had the other sheep for company. She was nice enough, though, and respectful of Lila. Still, Lila missed Ima. She sometimes found Ima's tracks or the tracks of her mighty consort, and almost every year she found a single new set of tracks whose scent reminded her of Ima's. Whenever Lila found a set of tracks that had to do with Ima, she would mark the spot and scratch the dirt so that Ima would recognize her sign if she passed that way again. She'd know that Lila was still thinking of her.

As for Yom and Lila, they lived on in service of the master. Sometimes the master placed a few new sheep in their care, and sometimes he took a few sheep away. What happened to the sheep he took they didn't know. Yom and Lila liked all the sheep well enough and minded them dutifully and carefully, although they couldn't teach them as Ima had.

As for love, though, Lila loved only Yom and Yom loved only Lila, especially after their first month together, when, drawn by the faint star fragrance that Yom found on Lila at that time of year, he fathered twin pups. Their love swelled instantly to include the newborns, but the pups didn't live. As before, the master found them and, for some incomprehensible human reason, drowned them in a basin of water.

What could Yom and Lila do? They couldn't help but

mate every year, and they couldn't help but have pups, sometimes three, sometimes four, once five. As her time of delivery drew near, Lila would find a place of shelter— a cedar thicket or a hollow under an overhanging rock— and then would keep her pups for as long as she could, pressing them with her thigh into the curve of her body, showing them only to Yom. He brought her food so that she could stay in hiding. But sooner or later the master would find her and take the pups. Then he and his wife would dispose of them, handing them over to human strangers or drowning them. The pain of her children's loss haunted Lila's dreams and never diminished, no matter how often she experienced it. But at least she had Yom to share her grief and to comfort her.

They had their good times too. Often they found a chance to play and would race around the hillsides together while the young sheep watched. Now and then they would find a dead deer or would rob a lynx of a carcass and eat their fill, an especially pleasant experience for Lila because the lynx in question was the large male who had claimed the upland pasture as his own on the night the star had first appeared. Lila didn't think the lynx should be there at all, and she delighted in treeing him and robbing him while he watched.

Now and then the dogs would fight battles with the wild wolves, battles that the dogs would win thanks mainly to Lila. But although Yom was smaller and not as strong, he fought at Lila's side with a will so pure that she was emboldened. He made her invincible, so certain of herself and of victory that she didn't feel her wounds. And back in the hills, the wolves knew it. Mostly they stayed away from Lila.

So the dogs had their share of joy and sorrow, of loss and triumph, all of which they experienced together. And at the very core of their beings they were grateful for that. Sometimes at night Lila looked for the star that had brought them together, remembering it with both awe and puzzlement. Of course, the star was long gone, far behind the sun. But Yom was not gone. He was right there beside her, and she beside him. Even in her sleep she could feel his body pressed against hers, their fur mingled. They belonged together and belonged to each other as surely as day follows night.

Do animals sense divinity? Clearly they do. They seem to respond to divinity as they see it, often as it is expressed by the sun. A solar eclipse, for example, seems to cause awe in birds who, as the sky darkens, sing their evening songs with such pauses and hesitations as to seem uneasy. Mammals grow still and often hide uncharacteristically until the sun returns.

But animals also note the daily movement of the sun, especially as it rises and sets, and respond to it as if they saw a relationship between it and them. Two wolves, now deceased (poisoned by a woman who assumed they were evil), made a practice of waiting side by side at the east window of their enclosure before dawn and would sing together the moment the red rim of the sun appeared. On cloudy days, when the sunrise wasn't visible, they didn't sing at dawn. In the same spirit, a lion in Namibia was observed staring fixedly at the western horizon, watching intently as the sun went under. Just before it vanished he roared at it or to it, as if he were communicating with another lion. Certain lions habitually roar in response to thunder, answering as if it were a familiar voice that had just called out to them.

And animals appear to appreciate natural beauty. In Idaho, in the geological formations called Silent City of Rocks, a puma spent his leisure hours on a ledge looking out at a view so vast that distant mountains were lost in haze. In Namibia on the Skeleton Coast, a small population of elephants who must climb a mountain to drink from a high spring habitually climb even higher to a lookout where there is a spectacular view. There they stand for long periods of time, rumps to the cliff that rises behind them, just gazing.

Surely it is our own animal nature that recognizes the divinity of the natural world in all its mystery and beauty, despite the distressing habits and limited perception that afflict our species. So perhaps our hope of redemption lies in the fact that we are animals, not that we are people. The force that makes the sun rise . . . the god whose voice we hear in thunder . . . the God of Abraham . . . Gaea . . . /Gao!Na . . . aren't these but a single entity? What other could they be?

Acknowledgments

In a book of this kind the illustrations are fully as important as the writing, and I am very thankful and grateful that my words could be accompanied by these particular woodcuts. I would like to express my appreciation to their creator, Andrew Davidson. I am also greatly indebted to the anthropologist Nancie Gonzalez. Nancie has spent much time in the Near East and generously shared her knowledge of that part of the world. I am equally indebted to my son, Ramsay Thomas, who has offered invaluable advice on the story. Whatever virtue this book may have is due in large part to him. I am also indebted to my very skilled editor, Becky Saletan, and to my splendid agent, Ike Williams. I am indebted to Katy Payne for her observation of elephants viewing a landscape. I am also indebted to Bruce Fox for generously helping with the cover photo.

I am indebted to a dingo, the late Viva, for demonstrating, by silently creeping under the skirt of my daughter's floor-length coat, how awesome a total eclipse of the sun is to dingoes. I am indebted to a husky, the late Coki, who was the model for Lila, and to a pariah dog in Namibia's Bushmanland named /Gau (Strong), the model for Yom, and to an alert young she-goat in Idaho whose name, if she had one, I never knew—the model for Ima.